LET'S CELEBRATE AMERICA

THE GRAND CANYON

This Place Rocks

by Joanne Mattern

RED
CHAIR
•PRESS•

Let's Celebrate America is produced and published by Red Chair Press:
Red Chair Press LLC   PO Box 333   South Egremont, MA 01258-0333
www.redchairpress.com

About the Author

Joanne Mattern is a former editor and the author of nearly 350 books for children and teens. She began writing when she was a little girl and just never stopped! Joanne loves nonfiction because she enjoys bringing history and science topics to life and showing young readers that nonfiction is full of compelling stories! Joanne lives in New York State with her husband, four children, and several pets.

Publisher's Cataloging-In-Publication Data
Names: Mattern, Joanne, 1963–
Title: The Grand Canyon : this place rocks / by Joanne Mattern.

Description: South Egremont, MA : Red Chair Press, [2017] | Series: Let's celebrate America
  | Interest age level: 008-012. | Includes a glossary and references for additional reading.
  | "Core content classroom."--Cover. | Includes bibliographical references and index. |
  Summary: "One of the most visited places in North America, Grand Canyon National Park
  is like an open window to Earth's geologic history. The carving of the canyon's walls by
  erosion left a cross-section of the Earth's crust from millions and millions of years ago. See
  for yourself how grand and beautiful this gorgeous gorge really is."--Provided by publisher.

Identifiers: LCCN 2016954992 | ISBN 978-1-63440-221-7 (library hardcover) |
  ISBN 978-1-63440-231-6 (paperback) | ISBN 978-1-63440-241-5 (ebook)

Subjects: LCSH: Grand Canyon (Ariz.)--Juvenile literature. | Geology--United States--Juvenile
  literature. | CYAC: Grand Canyon (Ariz.) | Geology--United States.

Classification: LCC F788 .M38 2017 (print) | LCC F788 (ebook) | DDC 979.1/32--dc23

Copyright © 2018 Red Chair Press LLC

Map and technical illustrations by Joe LeMonnier

Photo credits: p. 7, 17, 20, 21, 22, 24, 28: Dreamstime; p. 15, 29: National Park Service; cover, p. 1,
3, 5, 6, 7, 9, 10, 11, 12, 13, 14, 16, 18, 19, 23, 25, 26, 27, 30, 31, back cover: Shutterstock

Printed in the United States of America
0517 1P WRZF17

Table of Contents

A Place of Beauty

Look around. You are standing in one of the most amazing places on Earth. A huge crack in the land spreads out in front of you. Looking down, you see rocks that rise from the ground far below. Some of the rocks are flat on top. Others are jagged and sharp. The landscape is striped with different colors, and the rocks glow in the sun. Patches of green dot the ground and small, narrow **canyons** cut into the rocks. A sparkle of water shows a river flowing at the bottom of the canyon. From the top, the river looks small, but a closer look shows a noisy rush of water carving through the canyon floor.

This place is the Grand Canyon. It is millions of years old. It is one of the most beautiful places on Earth. The Grand Canyon is one of the Seven Natural Wonders of the World. It is the only Wonder located in the United States.

The seven natural wonders of the world

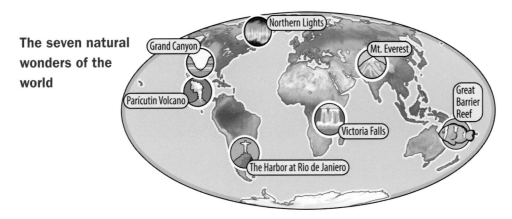

4

How Was the Grand Canyon Formed?

The Grand Canyon is in northern Arizona. The canyon is located on a large, flat area of land called the Colorado **Plateau**. The Grand Canyon is 277 miles (446 km) long. In some places it is 18 miles (29 km) wide and more than a mile (1.6 km) deep. The Grand Canyon is in the **desert**. The land here is very dry.

Yet, water formed the Grand Canyon. The Colorado River flows through the bottom of the canyon. Over millions of years, the water wore away the rocks around it. This process is called **erosion**. Wind and rain also cause erosion. Rain washes away bits of rock. Wind blows against the rocks and wears them away, one tiny piece at a time.

We learn much about nature, culture, and history of the Grand Canyon from this magnificent river.

Erosion by wind and rain creates beautiful rock formations in the canyon.

Erosion takes a long time. It has taken six million years for the Colorado River to carve the Grand Canyon out of the rocks. The movement of water created different shapes in the rocks. Some of the rocks are flat on top. These are called **mesas**. Some rocks are harder than others. If a rock is soft, it wears away more quickly than a rock that is hard. That is why the rocks in the Grand Canyon have different shapes.

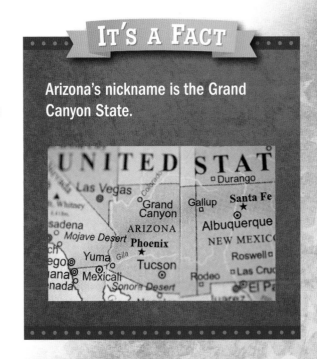

IT'S A FACT

Arizona's nickname is the Grand Canyon State.

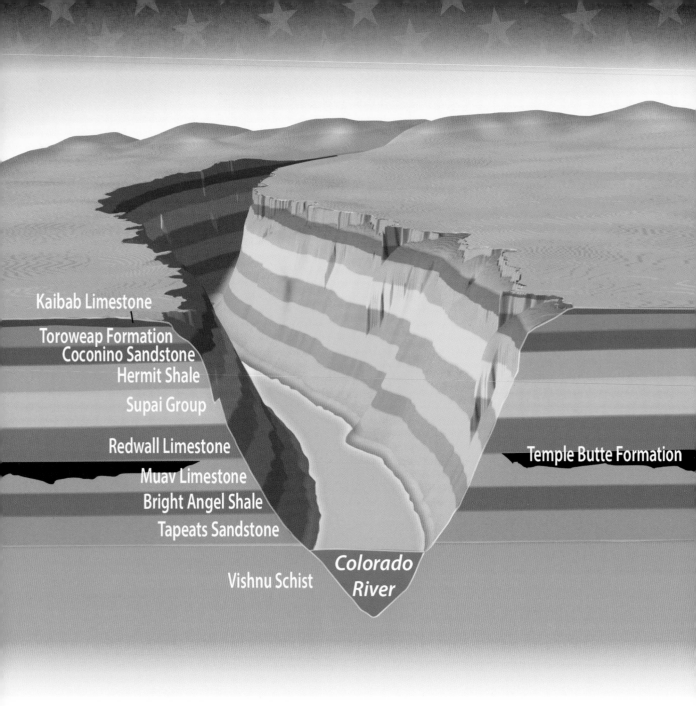

Kaibab Limestone

Toroweap Formation
Coconino Sandstone
Hermit Shale

Supai Group

Redwall Limestone

Temple Butte Formation

Muav Limestone

Bright Angel Shale

Tapeats Sandstone

Colorado
River

Vishnu Schist

There are different kinds of rock in the Grand Canyon. The rocks are also different colors. The color of a rock depends on the minerals it is made of. Some of the rocks are white limestone. There is also a type of red limestone. Limestone is soft and wears away easily.

At the bottom of the canyon you can see a dark rock called schist. **Sediment** created by sand and mud flowing in the Colorado River also turned into a type of rock called sandstone. You can see this red-colored rock near the bottom of the canyon. All in all, there are about eleven different layers of rock in the Grand Canyon.

World's Biggest?

The average depth of the Grand Canyon is about 1 mile (1.6 km). But the Yarlung Tsangpo Canyon in the Himalayas is the world's longest and deepest canyon. The widest? Capertee Valley Canyon in Australia at 18 miles (29 km) wide!

The rocks at the top of the canyon are young compared to the rocks at the bottom. The rocks at the top of the canyon are about 250 millions years old. The rocks at the bottom formed two billion years ago!

Nearly 40 rock layers are exposed in the Grand Canyon.

Parts of the Canyon

The Grand Canyon has three parts. The northern part is called the North Rim. The North Rim is the coldest and wettest part of the Grand Canyon. This area gets about thirty inches (46 cm) of rain and snow every year. Because it is so wet and cool here, this part of the Grand Canyon looks very different from the dry rocks and desert inside the canyon.

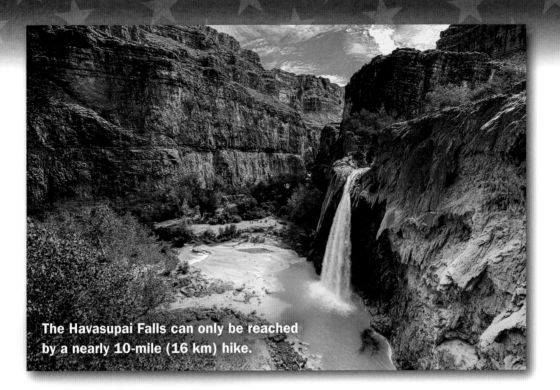
The Havasupai Falls can only be reached by a nearly 10-mile (16 km) hike.

The southern part of the Grand Canyon is called the South Rim. This is the part of the canyon that most people visit. There is a lot to see on the South Rim. Visitors can look down into the canyon's rocky depths. They can hike and camp. They can even travel down to the canyon floor.

The third part of the Grand Canyon is called the Inner Canyon. Here visitors can see the Colorado River up close. There are also many smaller streams at the bottom of the canyon. There are amazing sights deep inside the Grand Canyon, including waterfalls and smaller canyons.

IT'S A FACT

Scientists have found **fossils** of corals and sponges in the Grand Canyon. This tells us that the area was once covered by water.

The Colorado River and the Glen Canyon Dam

The Colorado River used to be much wilder than it is today. In 1963, workers built the Glen Canyon Dam upstream from the Grand Canyon. The dam reduced the amount of water flowing into the Colorado River. This means that the river does not cut into the rocks with as much force as it used to.

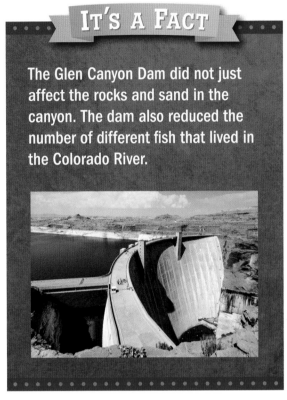

The river also does not carry as much mud and other sediments through the canyon. In the past, the Colorado River would flood every spring. The floodwaters carried sand into the Grand Canyon. The river left the sand and created beaches along the canyon floor. After the Glen Canyon Dam was built, sand no longer flowed down the river and the sand beaches disappeared.

The History of the Canyon

The Grand Canyon was here long before any people lived in the area. The first people to live near the canyon were Native Americans. Groups of hunters first came to the area at least ten thousand years ago. These groups were **nomads** who did not settle in the area. However, scientists have found stone spearheads in the area. The Native Americans used these spearheads to hunt large animals, such as bighorn sheep and deer.

Native American pictographs found on a cave wall inside the Grand Canyon

More than two thousand years ago, another group of nomads came to the Grand Canyon. They were called the Desert Culture. These hunters made figures of animals out of tree twigs that they bent and twisted together. Scientists have found many of these figures in caves in the Grand Canyon's walls.

A group of Native Americans called the Anasazi came to the Grand Canyon about 1,500 years ago. They hunted and farmed. About 700 years ago the Anasazi moved away and other native tribes moved in. These new tribes included the Hopi, the Navajo, and the Southern Paiute. These tribes hunted and also herded sheep.

In 1933, split-twig figurines were first discovered in caves within the Grand Canyon.

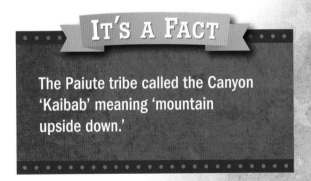

IT'S A FACT

The Paiute tribe called the Canyon 'Kaibab' meaning 'mountain upside down.'

Grand Canyon Skywalk

The Hualapai, meaning "People of The Tall Pines," are native people of the Southwest and still live near the Grand Canyon today. Traditionally hunter-gatherers, the Hualapai once lived in an area of more than 5 million acres. Their homeland stretched from the Grand Canyon south to the Santa Maria River and from the Black Mountains east to the pine forests of the San Francisco peaks. The Hualapai Reservation, created in 1883, is nearly 1,000,000 acres that includes 108 miles (174 km) of the Colorado River and Grand Canyon. Today there are approximately 2,100 enrolled members of the Hualapai Tribe and nearly half live in Peach Springs, AZ, the capital of the Hualapai Nation. Years of social and economic hardship led Hualapai Leaders to take measures that would lead to an independent future for the generations to come. As a result, the Hualapai decided to open their land to visitors in 1988, creating Grand Canyon West as a tourism destination.

In 2007, the Hualapai built a unique observation deck. The Skywalk, managed by the Hualapai Tribe and located on tribal lands, consists of a horseshoe shaped steel frame with glass floor and sides that projects about 70 feet (21 m) from the canyon rim. It's an amazing view—for the brave at heart!

The maximum occupancy for the Skywalk is 120 people at one time.

 During the 1500s, Spanish explorers came to North America. Francisco Coronado sent some of his men to explore the Grand Canyon. These men were the first Europeans to see the canyon. They tried to climb to the bottom, but it was too hard to get down the giant rocks, so they had to give up. About 200 years later, two Spanish priests saw the Grand Canyon while they were traveling with a group of soldiers. One of them named the canyon's river the Colorado. "Colorado" is the Spanish word for "red." The river looked red because of all the sand it was carrying.

IT'S A FACT

Lieutenant Ives sent a report back to Washington, D.C. In it, he said the Grand Canyon was "of course, altogether valueless."

After a war with Mexico, the United States won control of the area around the Grand Canyon in 1848. In 1857, the U.S. government sent some explorers to the Colorado River. The trip did not go well. The leader of the group was Lieutenant Joseph Christmas Ives. He wrecked his ship in the waters of the Colorado River.

In 1869 a man named John Wesley Powell decided to travel down the Colorado River from one end to the other. Powell was a geologist, or a scientist who studies rocks. He took notes about everything he saw during the trip. Powell and his men sailed down the dangerous **rapids** of the Colorado River. The trip was very dangerous. Many men left the group before Powell finally reached the western end of the Grand Canyon on August 29, 1869.

Mexican-American War

The Mexican-American War (1846-1848) marked the first U.S. armed conflict chiefly fought on foreign soil. It pitted a politically divided and unprepared Mexico against the administration of U.S. President James K. Polk, who believed the United States had a "manifest destiny" to spread the U.S. territory across the continent to the Pacific Ocean. A border skirmish along the Rio Grande River started off the fighting and was followed by a series of U.S. victories. When the dust cleared, Mexico had lost about one-third of its territory, including nearly all of present-day California, Utah, Nevada, Arizona and New Mexico.

Most of the war was fought on Mexico's territory.

Powell made several trips to the Grand Canyon. He wrote about his trips and also gave public talks. Other people made the trip to visit the canyon. In 1901, a railroad was built to the area of the canyon. Hotels and restaurants were built too. In 1919, more than 40,000 tourists visited the Grand Canyon. That same year, the Grand Canyon became part of the **National Park** System. No one is allowed to build in the park, and the government is in charge of protecting this natural wonder.

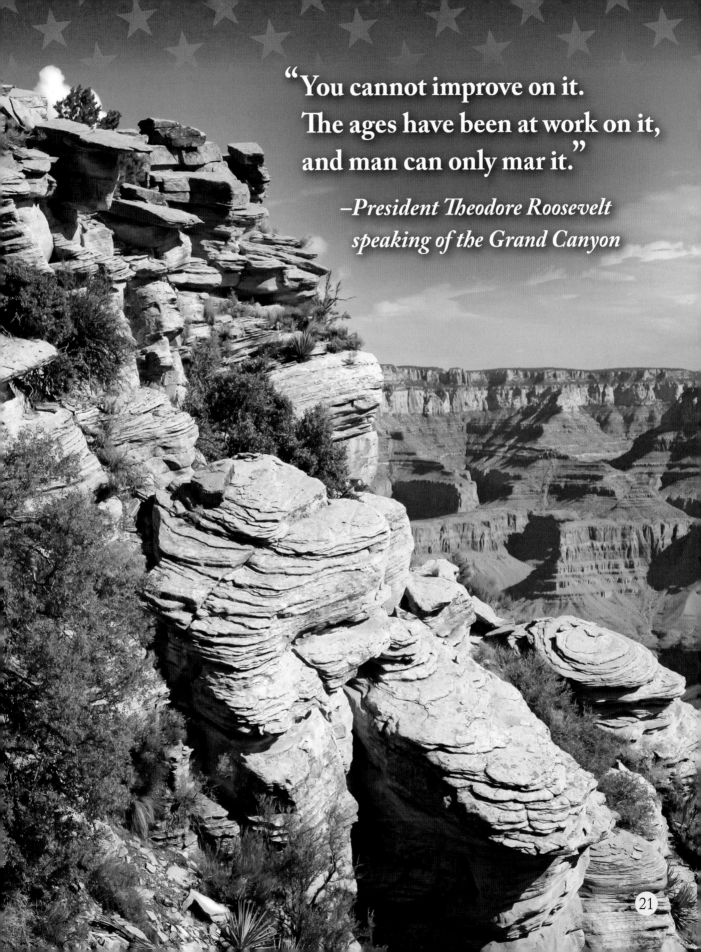

"You cannot improve on it. The ages have been at work on it, and man can only mar it."

–President Theodore Roosevelt
speaking of the Grand Canyon

21

Canyon Life

It is not easy to live in the Grand Canyon. The area is a desert, which means there is little water. Temperatures can soar over 100 degrees F (38° C) during the day, and drop below freezing at night. Despite these harsh conditions, many plants and animals live in the canyon.

More than 1,500 different kinds of plants live in and around the Grand Canyon. Pine, fir, and aspen trees grow along the cooler, wetter North Rim. There are grasslands and meadows filled with wild flowers in this area as well.

Deep inside the canyon, the ground is too dry for trees to grow. Instead, the most common plant here is the cactus. A cactus stores liquid inside its trunk and has long roots that can soak up water from deep underground. The Inner Canyon also has sagebrush, manzanita, and yucca plants.

IT'S A FACT

A visitor to the Grand Canyon can pass through dozens of climate zones in one day.

Many animals live in the Grand Canyon as well. Elk, deer and bighorn sheep climb the rocks. Bobcats and mountain lions hunt for smaller prey, such as mice, rabbits, and ground squirrels. Hawks, golden eagles, and condors also swoop down to catch their prey. Other birds, such as cormorants, great blue herons, and sandpipers eat the fish that swim in the Colorado River.

The Grand Canyon is also home to more than fifty species of reptiles and amphibians. Reptiles include smaller lizards such as the gecko. Geckos are active at night, when it is cooler. Nighttime is when they catch insects. During the hot day, they hide under rocks where it is cool. Other lizards, such as the chuckwalla, don't mind the high temperatures. They are active during the day. Chuckwallas eat flowers and leaves. These big lizards get all of the water they need from the plants they eat.

During the warmer months, California condors are seen regularly from the South Rim.

The most dangerous animal in the park is the rock squirrel. Every year, dozens of visitors are bitten when they try to feed these animals.

Visiting the Grand Canyon

More than five million people visit the Grand Canyon each year. There are many activities to do there. In fact, the Grand Canyon is so big and there is so much to see that people visit the canyon many times and still cannot see all of it.

Most visitors start at the South Rim. Visitors can stand at the top of the canyon and look at the amazing view. One of the best spots to look at the canyon is called Mather Point. People can also ride **mules** down trails into the park. Visitors can take short rides along the trails near the rim. Or they can stay in the canyon overnight. People hike or camp in the canyon. There are many trails to explore and amazing things to see.

Tourists ride mules in the Grand Canyon.

Many people like to explore the Colorado River. Guides take visitors on white-water rafting trips down the river. They paddle large rafts through the rough water. Seeing the Grand Canyon from the river at the bottom is very different than looking down from the top!

River rafting trips take visitors through the heart of the Grand Canyon.

Protecting the Grand Canyon

The Grand Canyon is part of the U.S. National Park System. Lands in the park system are protected. People cannot build inside the park or damage any of the natural resources there.

Because the Grand Canyon is such a popular tourist site, the National Park Service has taken steps to protect the land there. People cannot drive up to the canyon because so many cars would pollute the air. Instead, visitors leave their cars farther away. They take buses to the South Rim. People also have to make reservations to camp in the Grand Canyon or take rafting trips down the Colorado River. These rules allow the Park Service to control how many people are in the canyon at one time. Park **rangers** also patrol the area. They pick up litter and make sure everyone follows the rules. Their job is to keep both visitors and the canyon safe.

The Grand Canyon can also help us understand how small our role is in the larger world. Standing on its rim and thinking about the millions of years that have passed since the canyon was created gives visitors an appreciation of their place in the natural world.

Park rangers protect the land, animals, plants, artifacts, and visitors at the Grand Canyon.

Glossary

canyon: a deep, narrow river valley with steep sides

desert: a dry area

erosion: the process by which moving water or wind wears away rock over time

fossils: the remains of ancient organisms that are preserved in rock

mesas: broad, flat-topped hills with steep sides

mules: animals that are part horse and part donkey

national park: an area that is owned and managed by the government

nomads: people who travel from place to place instead of settling in one place

plateau: a high, flat piece of land

ranger: a person who works in a national park

rapids: fast-moving water in a river

sediment: pieces of dirt, mud, and rocks that are carried by water

Learn More in the Library

Books

O'Connor, Jim. *Where Is the Grand Canyon?*
Grosset & Dunlap, 2015.

Rau, Dana Meachen. *U.S. Landforms* (True Books).
Scholastic, 2012.

Vieira, Linda. *Grand Canyon: A Trail Through Time.*
Walker Children's Press, 2000.

Web Sites

The Hualapai Nation's Grand Canyon West

www.grandcanyonwest.com

National Park Service

www.nps.gov/grca/learn/kidsyouth/index.htm

Science Kids

www.sciencekids.co.nz/sciencefacts/earth/
grandcanyon.html

Index